THE ZOOPENDOUS SURPRISE

Written by **BOOTS HENSEL**

Illustrated by **ANDREA GABRIEL**

Enjoy These Titles from Pleasant St. Press

Off I Go!
New Old Shoes
That Kind of Dog
Little Shrew Caboose
Your Tummy's Talking!
The Warmest Place of All
On a Dark, Dark Night
My Sister, Alicia May
The Zoopendous Surprise
Farmer Brown and His Little Red Truck
If a Monkey Jumps Onto Your School Bus

Text copyright Carol Lynne Hensel © 2009
Illustrations copyright Andrea Gabriel © 2009

ISBN: 978-0-9792035-5-8
Library of Congress Control Number: 2008924635

10 9 8 7 6 5 4 3 2 1

Printed and bound in the USA

Published by Pleasant St. Press
PO Box 520
Raynham Center, MA 02768 USA

www.pleasantstpress.com
e-mail: info@pleasantstpress.com

Book Design by Jill Ronsley, suneditwrite.com

In loving memory of my daughter, Courtney, the inspiration for this book and Mary and Ellen's keeper until her death in 2004. Courtney, you continue to inspire me every day. And for my husband, Larry, and daughter, Kimberly, for their unfailing encouragement and love.

– BH

With utmost love to Diane and Bruce Hall, my parents and tireless encouragers.

– AG

The author wishes to thank the Little Rock Zoo in Arkansas and
Mary and Ellen's present keepers, Britt, Charity and Jayne,
for the trunk-loads of information they provided for this book.
A portion of the author's royalties will be donated to the Little Rock Zoo.

"We have a surprise today," the zookeepers whisper. "Shhh! Don't tell the elephants!"

Mary and Ellen, the Asian elephants, overhear the whispering. "A surprise!" says Mary, twirling her tail. "What can it be?"

The elephants watch the zookeepers carry a big box into the zoo.

"What's in that box?" Ellen says. She stretches her trunk high in the air to sniff the surprise. Smells of cotton candy and roasted peanuts drift by, tickling her nose–but that's no surprise.

Mary touches the ground with her trunk. Does the earth rumble, giving her a clue? Only her tummy rumbles! That's no surprise.

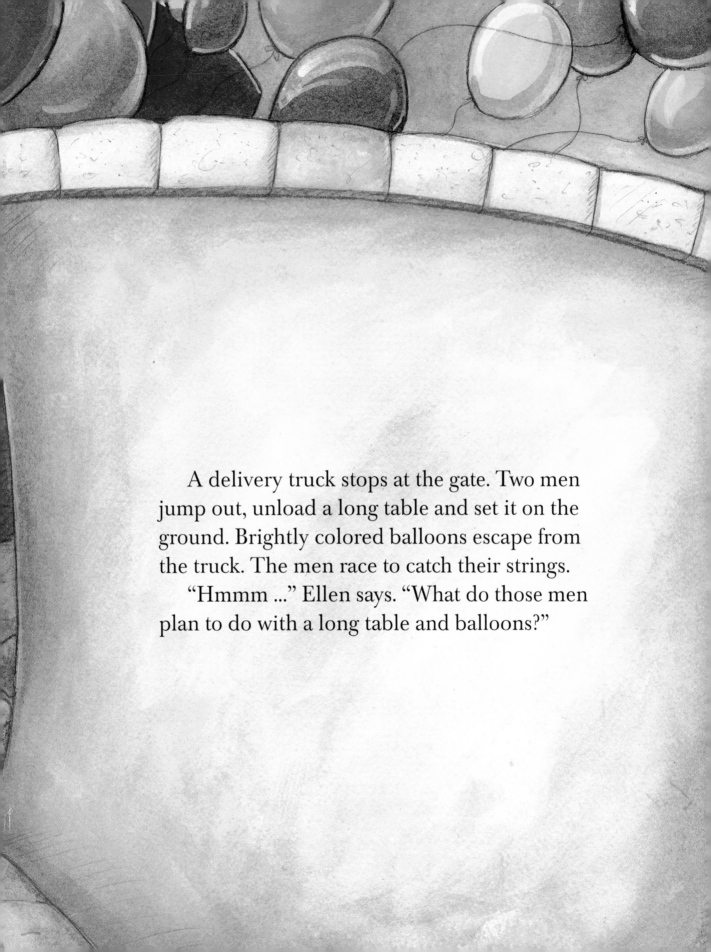

A delivery truck stops at the gate. Two men jump out, unload a long table and set it on the ground. Brightly colored balloons escape from the truck. The men race to catch their strings.

"Hmmm ..." Ellen says. "What do those men plan to do with a long table and balloons?"

The elephants are eager to take their walk.

Today, gentle Mary won't lag behind, the way she sometimes does. Mischievous Ellen won't sneak bites of bamboo, the way she usually does.

Both elephants are eager to visit the other animals and ask if they know about the surprise.

On their walk, they meet Mahale the chimpanzee. This chatty chimp often knows what's new at the zoo before the other animals do.

"Excuse me, Mahale," says Ellen.
"Do you know about the surprise?"

Mahale stops swinging just long enough to
reply. "Yes, I do, but it's a surprise and I can't tell
you." She smiles, reaches for a branch and, with
one swoop, disappears in the green canopy above.

Lumbering down the path, the elephants encounter BJ the giraffe. He has a very long neck, so he can look far across the zoo.

BJ is busy plucking tasty leaves from a treetop with his long black tongue. "Excuse me, BJ," says Mary. "Have you seen the surprise?"

"Yes, I have, but I can't tell. It's a surprise!" says BJ, and he returns to his green leafy breakfast.

Farther down the path, Nyla and Sydney the lions lounge in the morning sun. When they see the elephants, they greet them with loud roars.

Mary and Ellen hear the sound, and their big wrinkly legs shake. Summoning their courage, they ask together, "H-h-h-have you seen the surprise?" But just like Mahale and BJ, the lions reply, "We can't tell you. It's a surprise!"

Disappointed, Mary and Ellen make one last attempt to find out what the surprise could be. They ask Einstein, the wise old owl.

"Excuse me, Einstein," says Mary. "Do you know about the surprise?"

Einstein hoots at his curious visitors. "Of course, I know! I'm a wise owl," he says. "But I can't tell. It will ruin the surprise."

He turns his head and snuggles into his feathers.

Mary and Ellen lumber home just in time for a bath. They spray each other until they are soaked from trunk to tail. Sometimes they playfully spray their zookeepers, but not today.

With tails and ears drooping, the elephants are about to give up.

As they bend their knees to lie down for a nap,
Mary spots something at the far end of their enclosure.

Colorful balloons!

Her eyes sparkle. She notices the table that the men carried off the truck earlier in the day. It's piled high with watermelons, peanuts, loaves of bread and their favorite food of all—green jiggly Jell-O. On one end is the big box that the zookeepers were carrying that morning.

Mary and Ellen trumpet with delight! Then they see their zookeepers opening the big box.

"Surprise!" cry the zookeepers.

"A birthday cake!" Ellen shouts.

The elephants' tails swish and their
ears flap back and forth as their friends sing
"Happy Birthday!" Mary and Ellen make a
wish, blow out the candles and happily eat the
scrumptious cake.

Later, with their tummies full of goodies, Mary and Ellen hear the calls of their friends.

"What did you wish for?" screeches Mahale.

"Yes! We want to know!" cries BJ.

"Tell us your wish!"
roar Nyla and Sydney.

"Tell! Tell!"
hoots Einstein.

Mary and Ellen hook their tails together and flap their ears.
They are as happy as two elephant friends can be.
"We can't tell!" they trumpet. "It's a surprise!"